ONCE UPON A FAIRY TALE

The Magic Mirror

STORY BY
**Anna
Staniszewski**

ART BY
**Macky
Pamintuan**

BRANCHES

SCHOLASTIC INC.

ONCE UPON A FAIRY TALE

Read all of Kara and Zed's adventures!

TABLE OF CONTENTS

For Lia — AS
For Ali, my brave princess — MP

Library of Congress Cataloging-in-Publication Data

Names: Staniszewski, Anna, author. | Pamintuan, Macky, illustrator.
Title: The magic mirror / by Anna Staniszewski ; illustrated by Macky Pamintuan.
Description: First edition. | New York : Scholastic Inc., 2019. | Series: Once upon a fairy tale ; 1 | Summary: The Ice Princess's magic mirror is broken, one piece is missing, and without it the Enchanted Kingdom is locked in a terrible, unseasonable, heat wave (even the palace is melting); two children, Kara and Zed, are determined to help, but first they must figure out whether the break is the result of the sibling rivalry between the Ice Princess and her sister the Sun Princess—or did the monkey do it? Identifiers: LCCN 2018053890| ISBN 9781338349719 (pbk.) | ISBN 9781338349733 (hardcover) Subjects: LCSH: Magic mirrors—Juvenile fiction. | Magic—Juvenile fiction. | Princesses—Juvenile fiction. | Sisters—Juvenile fiction. | Sibling rivalry—Juvenile fiction. | Monkeys—Juvenile fiction. | Fantasy. | CYAC: Mirrors—Fiction. | Magic—Fiction. | Characters in literature—Fiction. | Princesses—Fiction. | Sisters—Fiction. | Monkeys—Fiction. | LCGFT: Fantasy fiction. Classification: LCC PZ7.S78685 Mag 2019 | DDC 813.6 [Fic] —dc23 LC record available at https://lccn.loc.gov/2018053890

10 9 8 7 6 5 4 3 2 1   19 20 21 22 23

Printed in China   62
First edition, September 2019
Illustrated by Macky Pamintuan
Edited by Erin Black
Book design by Sarah Dvojack

1

Heat Wave

"**K**ara! The carriage is here!" Kara's mother called.

"Coming!" Kara called back. She peeled herself up off the storeroom floor. It was the only cool spot she could find in the shoe shop where her family lived and worked.

Kara tucked one last book into her bag and handed it to her father. He almost dropped it. "What did you pack in here?" he asked.

"Books," Kara said. "And maps. And more books."

"You're staying with your best friend for two days. Do you plan to read the whole time?" her mother asked.

"Yes! It's too hot to do anything else," Kara said. She went to the cottage door. It might as well have been an *oven* door. When she opened it, a wave of hot air entered the store.

It was late fall, but the Enchanted Kingdom had been in a heat wave for weeks. Humans, ogres, mermaids, and all the other creatures in the land were miserable. Kara had even heard that the witch's gingerbread house had melted!

"We should get going," Kara's mother said. Her parents would drop her off at her sleepover on their way to a shoe fair.

Kara climbed into the carriage and squeezed between the boxes of shoes her parents had packed for the fair.

The carriage left the village and rode past Wishing Pond. It hadn't rained in weeks, so there was barely any water.

Soon they came to the cottage where Kara's best friend Zed lived with his grandmother. Zed was in the garden, picking cherries. Or maybe just eating them. His face was smeared with red.

"Have fun!" Kara's parents called out as they rode away.

Kara went over to Zed. "Isn't it too hot to be out in the sun?" she asked.

"No, this weather is great!" Zed said. "Look at all this food! Gram says I can eat as many cherries as I want. Do you want some?"

Kara rolled her eyes. Nothing bothered Zed as long as his belly was full.

"No, thanks." She plopped down in a shady spot to read a book.

But a minute later, Zed yelled, "Nina, no! Don't chew on that!" He ran over to his old pet goat.

Nina had pulled rolls of paper out of Zed's bag. Zed was a royal messenger. He delivered letters for the princes and princesses of the land.

"What's this?" Kara asked, picking up a scroll. Someone had written RETURN TO SENDER on it in red letters.

Zed shrugged. "A message for Prince Patrick," he said. "I tried delivering it to him, but he sent it back."

Kara studied the wax seal. It was a crown of icicles. She recognized it from a book she'd read about the Enchanted Kingdom's royal families.

"Aspen!" she cried.

"Bless you," Zed replied.

"No! Aspen, the ice princess. This message is from her," Kara explained. "It looks important. Maybe we should open it."

"We can't!" Zed cried. "Royal messengers are *not* allowed to open the messages they carry. I could lose my job."

But Kara wasn't listening. The wax seal on the scroll had melted in the heat. The paper was open, begging her to look inside.

Kara read the message and gasped.

"What does it say?" Zed asked.

"The ice princess is in trouble!" she cried.

Dear Prince Patrick,

I send you greetings from the Ice Palace, and my apologies for how mean I was at our last fancy ball. I was grouchy because of all the heat.

As you know, it is my job to make winter happen each year with my ice magic. I must ask for your help in fixing my magic mirror. Without the mirror, I can't use the ice magic.

2
Summer Forever?

"**W**hat do you mean the ice princess is in trouble?" Zed asked.

Kara reread the message from Princess Aspen. "The letter says her magic mirror is broken! She can't make it snow without her mirror." Kara shook her head. "No wonder it has been so hot lately!"

"I like the heat," Zed said. "More sun means more food."

"For now. But more sun also means less rain," Kara said. "Look at those tomato plants. Their leaves are yellow. If it stays summer forever, *everything* will dry up."

Zed's eyes widened. "All our food will dry up, too?" he asked.

Kara nodded. "That's why we have to help Princess Aspen and save our kingdom!"

"What do we know about fixing magic mirrors?" Zed asked.

"Not much," Kara admitted. "But someone needs to help."

"You *always* want to go on adventures!" Zed said with a groan.

"Come on. I bet your gram won't mind," Kara urged.

As if by magic, Gram came outside. "Mind what?" she asked.

"The two of us want to go on an adventure," Kara said.

Gram smiled and said, "That's what young people are *supposed* to do. I'll go pack snacks for your big adventure!" She went back inside.

"See?" Kara said. "Your gram thinks we should go."

"But we don't know where the Ice Palace is," Zed said.

Kara pulled a map out of her bag. "Here, look. It's less than half a day's walk. If we leave now, we'll be there in time for dinner."

Zed's eyes widened. "Do you think they eat ice cream at the *Ice* Palace?"

"I bet they do!" Kara said.

Barely a minute later, Zed's bag was packed. There was a crow sitting on his shoulder.

"Is that bird coming with us?" Kara asked.

"Rooster can come if he wants," Zed said.

"What about Nina?" Kara asked. The goat loved to follow Zed around.

"Nah. She doesn't like the cold," Zed said. "We shouldn't take her to an ice palace."

Gram came out of the cottage with sacks of food. "This should last Zed until lunchtime," she said with a wink. "Have fun, you two."

As they set off, Kara's head buzzed with excitement. She was finally going on an adventure!

3
To the Ice Palace

As a royal messenger, Zed was used to traveling far and wide to deliver letters. But he was not a good traveler.

As they walked along the road, Zed kept stopping to fix his shoes or have a snack.

"I think it's time for a nap," he said when they paused for the fourth time.

"We'll be there soon," Kara said, pulling him along. But it didn't feel as though they were near the Ice Palace. The air was still hot and there was no sign of snow.

Finally Kara spotted four towers in the distance. They were sharp and shiny, like a giant fork aimed at the clouds.

"Look! It's Aspen's palace!" Kara said, pointing.

"Wow," Zed said. "I didn't think it would really be made out of *ice*."

The palace was sagging like a snowman in the sun.

"It's melting," Kara said.

"Do you think their ice cream is all right?" Zed asked, sounding worried.

"We better hurry," Kara said.

After that, the journey went much faster. The air grew cool and dry. Soon they were crunching through slushy snow.

When they got to the palace, Kara could see that its walls were frosty blocks of ice. She could almost see through them. A big green wall stood on the other side of the palace. *Did someone build that to protect the Ice Palace from the sun?* Kara wondered.

Zed knocked on the palace door, and it swung open.

A guard pulled Zed and Kara inside. "Hurry! Before a chunk of ice falls on you!" he said.

Inside, the palace was gray and cold. The hot sun, which barely shone through the ice walls, felt far away.

The place was cramped with guards. They were tall and stooped, with pale skin and blue eyes. They wore thick coats and gloves. Kara had never seen trolls like them before. They looked as if they'd been carved from ice. Then she realized they were *winter* trolls! She had only read about them in books.

Two of the guards searched Kara's bag.

"Hey, don't touch that!" Kara said as one of them sniffed her map.

Just then, a winter troll girl about Kara's age hurried through the door. She was dressed for summer, in shorts and a T-shirt.

"Out of my way!" the girl said. She had a large sack on her back.

She pushed past Kara and Zed and headed for the stairs. Suddenly, the sack on her back moved!

Kara wanted to ask what was inside, but the girl was already gone.

4

Princess Aspen

"Did you see that?" Kara asked Zed, staring after the winter troll girl.

"See what?" Zed asked. "The princess?"

"What princess?" Kara asked.

"Her!" Zed pointed.

Kara turned and gasped. A woman in a swirling white dress strolled toward them. A crown of icicles sat on her head. It seemed to be melting.

Kara couldn't believe it. She was in the same room as a *real princess*!

Zed sunk into a low bow. Kara followed his lead. He'd been around royalty a lot more than she had.

"Hello, Princess Aspen," Kara said. "We are here because we heard about your broken mirror."

"We've come to help!" Zed added.

"Is this a joke?" Princess Aspen asked. Water from her crown dribbled onto her forehead.

"What do you mean?" Kara said.

"I've asked every king and queen for miles around to help. And they've sent two *children* and a *pigeon*?" the princess asked with a glare.

"He's a crow. His name is Rooster," Zed said.

"And no one sent us," Kara said. "We came on our own."

That made Aspen glare more. She turned to leave.

"Your Highness, wait!" Kara called out. "We've come all this way. Could we at least see the magic mirror?"

The princess sighed. "Fine," she said. "Follow me. But don't touch anything."

Kara nodded as Zed put his hands in his pockets. Then they followed Princess Aspen up the icy staircase.

5

Scene of the Crime

Princess Aspen led Kara and Zed to her bedroom at the top of the stairs. It took Kara a moment to notice the monkey on Aspen's bed. But Zed spotted it right away.

"Who's that?" he asked. The monkey was asleep on Aspen's pillow.

Princess Aspen ignored Zed. She pointed to a wall by her door. "The mirror was here."

"Kara," Zed whispered. "That's a snow monkey! A *real* snow monkey!"

Kara shushed him as she listened to the princess.

"I found the mirror on the floor. It was smashed," Aspen said.

"Smashed?" Kara repeated. She'd hoped the mirror was only cracked.

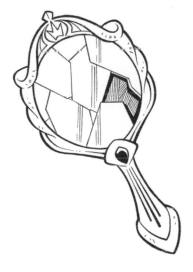

"A guard and I tried to put it back together," Aspen said. She lifted a silver mirror off a table. "But one piece of glass is missing. Without it, I can't use the mirror to call the cold and snow to the Enchanted Kingdom."

Kara shook her head. The mirror couldn't stay broken. Then summer would last forever. Everything would dry up!

Zed reached out to pet the monkey.

"Get away from him!" Aspen called across the room.

Zed jumped back. "Sorry," he said. "Your monkey is just so . . . snowy."

"His name is Clyde," Princess Aspen said.

At the sound of his name, Clyde opened his eyes.

Zed let out an excited gasp. "Come here, Clyde," he said, holding out his arm.

But Clyde turned away and hopped onto Aspen's shoulders. He settled around her neck like a scarf.

Zed sighed. Kara felt bad for him. Usually Zed was an animal magnet. But they had to focus on fixing the mirror and saving the kingdom.

"Your Highness, do you know who would want to break the magic mirror?" Kara asked.

Aspen laughed. "Oh, I *know* who broke it," she said.

Who Broke the Mirror?

Kara and Zed stared at the princess. "You know who broke the mirror?" they said together.

"Yes. It was my sister, Sola, the sun princess," Aspen said. "She loves hot weather. I bet she took the last piece so that the mirror would never work again."

"What makes you think she did it?" Kara asked.

"This room is protected with a magic spell," Aspen explained. "Only Sola is powerful enough to get inside. Besides, my sister and I have never gotten along."

"Are you *sure* your monkey didn't break the mirror?" Kara asked.

Aspen and Zed both gasped.

"Of course I'm sure!" Aspen said. "Clyde is a good boy." She scratched the monkey's belly.

Kara cleared her throat. "I'd like to talk to your sister. Where can we find her?" Kara didn't remember seeing Sola's palace on the map.

"Kara," Zed whispered. "I know we have to save the kingdom. But we haven't had ice cream yet!"

"Later," Kara whispered back.

"The journey will take no time at all," Aspen said. She pointed out the window. "Sola lives there."

Kara and Zed looked out at the giant wall by the palace. Did the sun princess live inside it? Then Kara saw something *over* the wall. A hint of green. A dash of brown. A twinkle of gold.

"There's a huge tree on the other side of that wall!" Zed said.

"That's not a tree," Kara realized. In between the branches she could make out windows and towers and doors. "It's the Sun Palace."

To the Sun Palace

Soon after Kara and Zed left Aspen's palace, they came to a group of ice statues. Each one had a look of surprise on its face.

"Princess Aspen has strange taste in art," Zed said.

Kara shivered, and it wasn't from the cold.

"There's something not right about these statues," she said.

They kept walking toward the giant green wall. As they got closer, they realized it was made of vines, not stone.

Kara's eyes widened as she reached out to touch the vines. "This wall must have been built with magic," she said.

"Look!" Zed said, pointing. "I think that's a door."

Zed was right. There was a small gate hidden in the wall of vines.

Kara opened it, and she and Zed stepped into another world.

The Sun Palace stood in the distance. Birds were singing. Flowers were blooming. The sun was shining. And shining. And shining.

"It's so hot I think my hair is sweating," Kara said.

When they got to the Sun Palace, the door was wide open. There were no guards in sight.

"Hello! Is anyone home?" Zed called as they went in.

"Welcome, friends!" someone said in a quiet voice.

In the corner was a young woman who had to be Aspen's sister. She looked almost exactly the same. But Sola wore a gold crown of flowers and a smile on her face. She was lying in bed, almost hidden in a pile of pillows.

"Your Highness," Kara said with a bow. "My name is Kara, and this is Zed."

Kara spotted a mirror
on the wall behind Sola.
It looked just like Aspen's
silver mirror. But this one
was framed in gold.

"Sorry I'm not getting
up," Sola said in a thin
voice. "Making it summer
all the time is exhausting."

Rooster fluttered toward Sola. He started
pecking at her sparkling crown.

"Rooster, no!" Zed cried. "Sorry. He likes
shiny things."

But Sola giggled and
held out her arm for
Zed's crow to sit on.
"What a lovely bird,"
she said. The sun
princess seemed a lot
nicer than her sister.

"Where is everyone?" Zed asked. Kara had been wondering the same thing. Aspen's palace had been bursting with guards. Here, dry leaves littered the floor and dust coated the furniture. No one had cleaned the Sun Palace in a long time.

"I'm alone," Sola said. "My sister froze all my guards months ago."

Kara remembered the surprised ice statues outside the wall. *They must've been Sola's guards!* she thought.

"Why would Aspen freeze your guards?" she asked the sun princess.

"She was angry at me for building the wall between our palaces," Sola said.

Aspen had said that she and her sister didn't get along, Kara remembered.

"Your Highness," Kara said. "We are here about Aspen's mirror. She—"

"She thinks you broke it," Zed cut in. "And she thinks you stole a piece from it so it could never be fixed."

"Zed!" Kara said.

But Sola didn't look upset. "Aspen is wrong," she said. "I would never break her magic mirror. Every year, I'm glad when she takes over for the winter. Then I can rest."

"But if *you* didn't break it, then who did?" Kara asked.

"I wish I knew," Sola said.

Just then, a loud screech echoed through the Sun Palace.

A Monkey to Share

Kara and Zed jumped at the loud screeching sound.

But Sola just smiled. "My monkey is back," she said.

"Does *everyone* have a monkey but me?" Zed huffed.

Sola whistled, and a snowy head popped through a window.

"Clyde!" Kara said. "I thought he was Aspen's monkey."

"Clyde was a gift from our parents," Sola explained. "They told us to share him. So he spends half his time at the Ice Palace, and half his time here." Clyde went to Sola and curled up in her lap. "Aspen says that I have Clyde more than half the time. But I feel like he's with Aspen more than me. It's not fair."

Kara almost laughed. Aspen and Sola were jealous of each other over a *monkey*?

The door to the palace creaked open. The troll girl from the ice palace peered in. She was wearing so many scarves and hats that Kara hardly recognized her.

"Clyde! Not again!" the troll girl said to the monkey.

"Kara, Zed, this is Rye," the princess said. "Rye takes care of Clyde at both palaces."

No wonder Rye was wearing summer clothes in the Ice Palace earlier. It must be tricky to switch between summer and winter all the time, Kara thought.

"I have to get Clyde back before Aspen sees he's gone," Rye said. She bowed to Sola. "If you don't mind, Your Highness."

Sola gave Clyde a pat on the head. "I will wait my turn," she said.

Rye clicked her tongue and held out an orange. Clyde ran over and grabbed the fruit.

"Good boy," Rye said.

"We should go back to the Ice Palace and look for more clues," Kara said.

"Good luck," Sola said. "I hope you find a way to fix Aspen's mirror soon." She let out a long, tired sigh.

Clyde darted out of the palace. Rye hurried after him.

"Hey, wait for us!" Zed called. He grabbed Kara's arm and pulled her out the door.

Princess of Shoes

Kara and Zed caught up to Clyde and Rye outside the Sun Palace. Zed offered to carry him, but the monkey hopped onto Kara's shoulders instead.

"I don't understand. Animals love me!" Zed said. Rooster gave him a little peck on the ear. "See?"

"Clyde only likes royalty. Are you a princess?" Rye asked Kara.

Kara laughed. "A princess of shoes, maybe."

The monkey felt heavier with each step Kara took. Soon Kara, Zed, Rye, and Clyde were back at the Ice Palace. They stopped outside the palace door.

They could hear Aspen slamming doors inside. "Where is Clyde?" she yelled to her guards.

"Should we bring him inside?" Zed asked.

Rye held out an empty sack. "Hop in," she told Clyde.

He leaped off of Kara's back and jumped inside.

Kara's mouth sagged open. *That's* what had been inside the moving sack she'd seen on Rye's back earlier! "You keep him in there?" she asked.

"It's the best way to get him into the palace without Aspen knowing he ran away," Rye said.

Aspen started yelling again.

"Please don't tell Aspen about this," Rye said. "Last time Clyde was missing, she had a fit. It was the same day the mirror broke. My ears are still ringing from all her yelling and slamming doors."

"We won't say anything," Kara said.

"Promise," Zed added.

Rye heaved the sack onto her back and hurried inside. Kara and Zed followed her.

"The princess said you were going to stay the night. Come," one of the guards told them. "Let me show you to your room. Your dinner is waiting for you there."

Kara and Zed exchanged excited looks. They were going to eat and sleep in the Ice Palace!

They followed the guard upstairs, but their excitement didn't last long. Their beds were made of hard ice and their pillows were stuffed with snow. Their blankets felt cold and damp.

Dinner was frozen fish slush. Zed ate three helpings. Kara and Rooster only pecked at their bowls.

While they ate, Kara and Zed went over what they had learned about the mystery of the broken mirror.

"Aspen thinks Sola broke her mirror," Kara said. "But I believe Sola. I don't think she did it."

"I agree," Zed said. "It's her job to keep the kingdom hot until it turns cold. Without Aspen's magic mirror, Sola has even more work to do."

"But if Sola didn't break the mirror, who did?" Kara asked.

Zed didn't have an answer.

"Don't worry," Zed told Kara as they got ready for bed. "In the morning we'll figure out how to fix the magic mirror."

"I hope so," Kara said. "I need to be back home tomorrow night, or my parents will worry."

Kara curled up on the hard, cold bed. Her mind was full of mirrors, monkeys, and princesses. But no matter how she tried to put them together, nothing added up.

An Icy Breakfast

In the morning, Kara had to climb out of a girl-shaped dent in the ice. She'd melted into the bed! Her whole body tingled with cold.

Zed looked colder than she felt. Even Rooster's beak was chattering.

"Breakfast will warm us up," Kara said. But when a guard brought them to the kitchen, they found only fish smoothies and fish ice pops.

"These are winter trolls' favorite foods," Gorda, the cook, explained.

"They're delicious!" Zed said, digging in.

Kara tried to be polite and sip her smoothie. "Yes, this food is really something," she choked. "So do you like working for Princess Aspen?"

Gorda chuckled. "Aspen has a temper, but we winter trolls can handle it. I only wish she and her sister would stop arguing."

"Are they really fighting over a monkey?" Kara asked.

"I know it sounds silly," Gorda said. "But the princesses never had to share anything before. I don't think they know how."

Zed's face lit up. "They should just give *me* the monkey!" he said. "Then they wouldn't have to fight anymore."

Gorda sighed. "I wish it were that easy. But until Aspen and Sola make peace, I'm afraid summer and winter will always clash."

"Do you know who put the magic mirror back together?" Kara asked. "Aspen said one of the guards helped her."

"Oh yes," Gorda said with a proud smile. "It was my daughter."

"Where can we find her?" Kara asked.

Gorda pointed toward a narrow staircase. "Up on the roof," she said.

11

Up to the Roof

"You said this adventure would be fun. This is *not* fun," Zed said as they scrambled across the slippery, icy roof. Zed clung to Kara like she was a life raft.

"Hello?" Kara called. "Is anyone up here?"

Someone grunted in response. It was Rye, the troll girl. Was *she* the cook's daughter?

"You shouldn't be up here!" Rye said. "You could fall."

Zed let out a little squeal.

"No one is falling," Kara insisted. "What are *you* doing up here?"

Rye pointed to a row of potted trees. "This is the only place that gets enough sun for my orange trees to grow," she said.

"Oranges? Yum!" Zed cried. "Can I have some?"

Rye shook her head. "They're for Clyde," she explained. "At the Ice Palace, he only wants to eat oranges. At the Sun Palace, he wants fish slush."

"Rye, we heard you helped Aspen put the magic mirror back together," Kara said.

"I tried," Rye said. "But it still wouldn't call the cold and snow."

"Are you sure you didn't just miss a piece?" Zed asked.

Rye nodded. "I used all the glass pieces that were there," she insisted. "Whoever left that footprint must have taken one."

"*What* footprint?" Kara and Zed asked together.

"When Aspen asked me to help her fix the mirror, I noticed a footprint in the middle of the broken glass," Rye said. "It looked as if someone had stepped in it."

Kara leaned in. "What did the footprint look like?" she asked. "Was it long or wide or round or pointy?"

"It was like any other footprint," Rye said with a shrug. Then she went back to her orange trees.

Kara sighed. She forgot other people didn't know as much about feet and shoes as she did. She paced around the rooftop, trying to think. But she was stumped.

"I don't know how we're going to find the missing piece of glass," Kara told Zed.

"Even if we find it, how will we put the mirror back together?" Zed asked. He tossed seeds on the ground for Rooster. The crow hopped around and pecked at them.

Maybe Zed was right. They knew nothing about fixing magic mirrors. Maybe they should give up and go home.

Crunch!

Kara stopped pacing. Some of Rooster's seeds were stuck to the bottom of her shoe. She brushed them off.

Just then, a guard came up the stairs. "Rye, Kara, and Zed," he announced. "Princess Aspen wishes to see you."

The Missing Piece!

When they got to the throne room, Aspen was sitting on a lumpy block of ice. Kara guessed that it had once been a chair. A sparkly ice chandelier hung overhead. Around them, guards mopped the melting floor.

"Have you solved the mystery of my broken mirror?" Aspen asked.

"Um, well, Your Highness," Kara said. "We've followed a few leads, but —"

At that moment, Rooster soared off Zed's shoulder and dived at Aspen's feet.

"Get that bird away from me!" Aspen shouted.

She kicked her feet, but Rooster kept pecking at Aspen's shoes.

As Zed tried to grab Rooster, Kara noticed something. Rooster wasn't pecking at the shiny buckles on the top of Aspen's shoes. He was pecking at the *soles*.

"Your Highness!" Kara cried. "I know what happened to the missing piece of the mirror!"

Aspen jumped to her feet. "What?"

"Rye said there was a footprint in the broken glass, like someone stepped in it," Kara explained. "I think the piece of glass got stuck to someone's shoe." *Just like the birdseed got stuck to mine,* she thought.

"Then go search Sola's shoes!" Aspen said.

"Your Highness, could we check yours first?" Kara asked.

"Mine?" Aspen sputtered.

Kara continued. "I think the footprint was yours," she said to Aspen. "You must have stepped in the glass when you first found the broken mirror."

Aspen lifted her foot. Sure enough, the piece of glass was stuck to the bottom of Aspen's shoe!

Kara plucked out the glass and put it in Aspen's hand.

The princess looked at it in surprise. "I can't believe it. All this time, the missing piece was under my foot," she said.

"Good job, Rooster!" Zed said, patting the crow's head.

"But I don't understand," Aspen said. "Who broke the mirror?"

"*You* did, Your Highness," Kara said.

13

Try, Try Again

"**T**hat's ridiculous!" Aspen cried. "Why would I break my own magic mirror?"

"It was an accident," Kara said. "You slammed your door, and the mirror fell."

Aspen opened her mouth to argue. Then she closed it again.

"Perhaps you're right," she said. Then her eyes lit up. "Now we can finally fix the mirror!"

Kara, Zed, and Rye got to work. But even though they had all the pieces, they couldn't fix the mirror.

"Try harder!" Aspen cried.

Rye brought a fresh block of ice, but the pieces wouldn't freeze together.

Kara tried a special shoe glue from her bag, but it wasn't strong enough.

"What if we asked Gorda to cook it?" Zed asked. "That might melt the glass."

But even in the hottest stew, the mirror stayed in pieces.

"Maybe only magic can fix it," Rye said finally.

"But I don't *have* magic without my mirror!" Aspen cried. Kara saw tears in her eyes. Maybe Aspen wasn't so different from her sister Sola after all.

Wait. Sola!

"Maybe Sola can use *her* magic mirror to help us," Kara said.

Aspen glared at her. "I won't ask my sister for help," the princess said.

"Why not?" Zed asked.

"Clyde likes Sola better," Aspen said with a sniff. "It was the same with our parents. She was their favorite, too."

At that moment, the ice chandelier crashed to the floor. Everyone dived for cover. Shards of ice rained over them.

Aspen brushed herself off. "Someone clean this mess. I'm going to my room!" she cried. Then she stormed away, calling for Clyde.

"Now what?" Zed asked.

"We have to get Sola and Aspen together," Kara replied. "And we need to hurry. This palace is crumbling around us!"

Zed nodded. "But how are we going to do that?" he asked.

"I have an idea," Kara said with a smile. "Rye, let Sola know we need her help. And Zed, I hope Rooster can crow *really* loudly."

Tricked

SQUAWWK!! Rooster crowed.

"Someone silence that bird!" Aspen cried. "It is time for Clyde's nap."

"Sorry, Your Highness. We can't make Rooster stop. We can't catch him," Zed said.

"He's outside on the wall," Kara said.

SQUAWWWWWWWWK!! Rooster crowed again, even louder.

Aspen huffed. "I will take care of this myself," she said. She stormed out of the palace. Clyde was at her side.

Kara and Zed hurried after them. When Aspen reached the wall, Sola stepped out of the small gate. She looked tired and weak, but she was smiling.

Aspen jumped back in surprise. "What are you doing here?" she asked.

"Sister, I can't keep summer going forever," Sola said. "Let me help you fix your mirror."

"Why would you help me?" Aspen asked. "Is it so everyone can say you're the nice one? The sunny one? The *warm* one?"

Clyde leaped out of Aspen's arms and ran over to Sola.

"See?" Aspen cried. "Everyone likes you better!"

Uh-oh. The plan wasn't going the way Kara had wanted. *The sisters have to apologize, not fight over the monkey again!* she thought.

Then something strange happened. Clyde grabbed both sisters' hands.

He pulled them forward until they were standing together. Then he hopped up and down in excitement.

Aspen and Sola jumped apart. But Clyde pulled them together again.

"What do you want us to do?" Sola asked.

"I don't understand," Aspen said.

But Kara understood. "He wants you to make up!" she said. "Your parents didn't want you to share Clyde by sending him back and forth between your palaces. They wanted you to take care of him *together*."

Zed's face lit up. "That's why he keeps running from palace to palace," he said. "He doesn't want to choose between you."

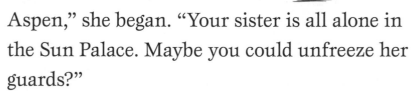

Clyde shrieked with excitement and jumped up and down again. Aspen and Sola looked at him in surprise.

Kara saw her chance. "Princess Aspen," she began. "Your sister is all alone in the Sun Palace. Maybe you could unfreeze her guards?"

Aspen frowned. "Only if she takes down that vine wall," she said.

"I have a better idea," said Sola. "What if I rebuild the wall into a house for Clyde? Then he won't have to choose between our palaces. We can both visit him there."

"He can't stay there alone," Aspen said. "Who will care for him?"

"I will!" Rye called out. "Please, Your Highnesses. I'm tired of being too hot and too cold all the time!"

"Then it's settled," said Aspen and Sola at once.

They looked at each other and smiled.

"I'm sorry I thought *you* broke my magic mirror," Aspen said to her sister. "Will you help me fix it?"

Rye hurried over with the broken mirror, and Aspen took it in her hands. Sola held out her own mirror and closed her eyes.

All in One Piece

As Kara watched, the gold mirror grew brighter and brighter. And then — *flash!* — a beam of golden light shot out. It hit the silver mirror, and the broken glass started to glow. When it cooled, everyone gasped.

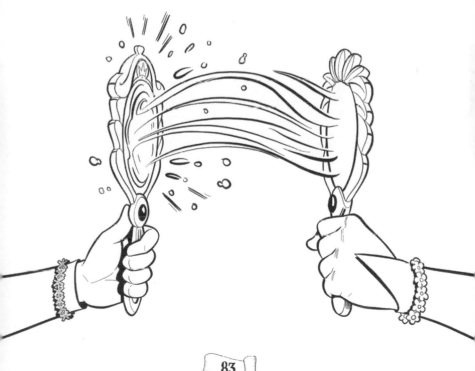

The silver mirror was all in one piece again!

Aspen hugged the mirror to her chest. "Thank you," she said to Sola. "I guess this is why Mom and Dad always liked you better."

"What?" Sola said. "No, they liked *you* better!"

The sisters laughed in surprise. Then they threw their arms around each other.

"See?" Zed said to Kara. "It all worked out. And it's a good thing Rooster came with us. We never would've found that missing piece without him!" He fed the crow some seeds.

"Good boy, Rooster," Kara said.

Clyde ran over and jumped onto Zed's shoulders.

Then he started eating seeds out of Zed's hand. Kara laughed at the look of joy on Zed's face. She knew how he felt.

Aspen turned to Kara and Zed. "Thank you," she said. "If there is anything I can do for you—"

"Your Highness," Zed broke in. "Maybe we could finally have some ice cream?"

"Zed!" Kara cried, rolling her eyes.

"What's ice cream?" Sola asked.

Zed grinned. "You're going to love it."

16
Ice Cream Feast

They all gathered in the kitchen where Zed helped the cook make an ice cream sundae feast. Kara was glad to eat something cold that did *not* taste like fish. As they ate, Aspen and Sola laughed and chatted like old friends. They even took turns feeding Clyde bites of ice cream.

When the feast was over, Aspen invited Kara and Zed to stay at the Ice Palace for as long as they wanted.

"Thank you, Your Highness," Kara said. "But it's time for us to head home."

Kara and Zed said their goodbyes.

Then they turned and started on the road for home. As they walked along the road, the sun hid behind the clouds. The air turned cool and crisp. Tiny flakes began to flutter from the sky.

"Look!" Zed cried. "It's snowing!" He caught a snowflake on his tongue.

Soon, snow covered the land.

Kara sighed happily. Their adventure had been a success. And summer was finally over.

Plop! A snowball landed on Kara's head.

"Hey!" Kara cried as Zed ran away. Kara grabbed a handful of snow. Then she chased Zed and Rooster along the road toward home.

ABOUT THE CREATORS

Anna Staniszewski is the author of over a dozen books for young readers, including *Secondhand Wishes* and *Dogosauraus Rex*. She lives outside of Boston with her family and teaches at Simmons University. She shares both Kara's love of reading and Zed's love of ice cream.

Macky Pamintuan was born in the Philippines. He received his bachelor of fine arts in San Francisco, and he has illustrated numerous children's books. He has a smarty pants young daughter who loves to read and go on imaginary adventures with her furry pal and trusty sidekick, Winter. He now lives in Mexico with his family.

The Magic Mirror

Questions and Activities

Why are Princess Aspen and Princess Sola fighting? What is one reason given in the story?

The Ice Palace and the Sun Palace are very different. What is life like at the Ice Palace? What is life like at the Sun Palace? Describe what makes each place special.

In chapter 12, Kara discovers an important clue. It tells her where the missing piece of the mirror is! What is the clue?

How does Clyde show Aspen and Sola that he does not like going between their two palaces? What solution do the princesses come up with so they can share Clyde?

Zed loves animals. Draw a picture of *your* favorite animal. Then write a few sentences explaining why you chose this animal.